ALVIN
AND
THE CHIPMUNKS™
CHIPWRECKED

THE JUNIOR NOVEL

HarperFestival is an imprint of HarperCollins Publishers.
Alvin and the Chipmunks: Chipwrecked: The Junior Novel
Alvin and the Chipmunks: Chipwrecked © 2011 Twentieth Century Fox Film Corporation and Regency Entertainment (USA), Inc. in the U.S. only. © 2011 Twentieth Century Fox Film Corporation and Monarchy Enterprises S.a.r.l. in all other territories.
Alvin and The Chipmunks, The Chipettes, and Characters TM & © 2011 Bagdasarian Productions, LLC. All Rights Reserved.
Printed in the United States of America.
No part of this book may be used or reproduced in any manner whatsoever without written permission except in the case of brief quotations embodied in critical articles and reviews.
For information address HarperCollins Children's Books, a division of HarperCollins Publishers, 10 East 53rd Street, New York, NY 10022.
www.harpercollinschildrens.com
Library of Congress catalog card number: 2011935479
ISBN 978-0-06-208658-7
11 12 13 14 15 LP/CW 10 9 8 7 6 5 4 3 2 1
❖
First Edition

FOX 2000 PICTURES AND REGENCY ENTERPRISES PRESENT A BAGDASARIAN COMPANY PRODUCTION A MIKE MITCHELL FILM "ALVIN AND THE CHIPMUNKS: CHIPWRECKED"
JASON LEE DAVID CROSS JENNY SLATE AND JUSTIN LONG MATTHEW GRAY GUBLER JESSE McCARTNEY AMY POEHLER ANNA FARIS CHRISTINA APPLEGATE
EXECUTIVE MUSIC PRODUCER ALI DEE THEODORE MUSIC SUPERVISOR JULIA MICHELS MUSIC BY MARK MOTHERSBAUGH EDITED BY PETER AMUNDSON PRODUCTION DESIGNER RICHARD HOLLAND DIRECTOR OF PHOTOGRAPHY THOMAS ACKERMAN, ASC
EXECUTIVE PRODUCERS KAREN ROSENFELT ARNON MILCHAN NEIL MACHLIS STEVE WATERMAN PRODUCED BY JANICE KARMAN ROSS BAGDASARIAN
BASED ON CHARACTERS CREATED BY ROSS BAGDASARIAN AND JANICE KARMAN WRITTEN BY JONATHAN AIBEL & GLENN BERGER DIRECTED BY MIKE MITCHELL
SOUNDTRACK ON
www.munkyourself.com

ALVIN
AND
THE CHIPMUNKS™
CHIPWRECKED

THE JUNIOR NOVEL

Based upon the characters
Alvin and the Chipmunks
created by **Ross Bagdasarian**
and **Janice Karman**

Screenplay by **Jonathan Aibel**
& **Glenn Berger**
Adapted by **Perdita Finn**

HARPER FESTIVAL
An Imprint of HarperCollins Publishers

ALVIN
AND
THE CHIPMUNKS™
CHIPWRECKED

THE JUNIOR NOVEL

Chapter 1

The Chipmunks scampered to the ramp of the cruise ship, singing. They were headed to the International Music Awards. But first they were going to enjoy a vacation together—at sea!

"One, two, three . . . one, two . . ." Dave, their manager and father, was carrying the tickets, the passports, and the suitcases. And he was trying to keep track of all of his chipmunks. "Guys, freeze," he ordered. They never seemed to stop dancing and moving.

The Chipmunks and their favorite girl band and best friends, The Chipettes, struck a pose. After all, they were famous music stars now. But where was Alvin?

At that exact moment a whiz of brown-and-white furry stripes slid down the railing of the cruise ship ramp—right into Dave's arms! What an entrance!

It was Alvin, of course. "Hey, Dave!" He leaned back, relaxed and cheerful as ever, and smiled up at him. "Where you been?"

Dave looked like he was about to explode in anger. "Where have *I* been? Trying to board the ship!"

"Already done that," chirped Alvin, putting his arms behind his head. "Also checked out our room, dibbed the side of the bed closest to the window, ordered us a round of virgin piña coladas, checked out some superfine ladies on your behalf, and signed us up for parasailing. You're welcome." He gave Dave a wink.

But Dave didn't acknowledge what Alvin had said. He'd only heard one word. *Parasailing*. There was no way he was going to let his little chipmunks fly high up into the air attached to a giant sail, protected by nothing more than a tiny harness. No way. It was too dangerous.

"There will be no parasailing. You're too

young," Dave announced firmly. "I know you want to have some fun on this cruise. But we need to set some rules about how we're going to behave on this ship."

Simon had been glaring at Alvin since he arrived. "Let's start with you can't call dibs on a bed until everyone's in the room!"

The Chipettes crowded around. "Yeah! Good rule! That's right!"

"Unfair!" added Theodore, nodding his head in agreement.

"Okay, there's rule number one," sighed Dave. "Should we go over the rest of them?"

"Don't worry, Dave," said Alvin sweetly. "Rules is my middle name." His whiskers twitched as he held back a mischievous smile.

Before Dave could say anything else, Alvin hopped out of his arms and led the other chipmunks up the ramp. Dave followed, shaking his head. This was going to be some trip. He could already tell. To top it all off, he thought he saw someone dressed as a giant pelican staring at him from across the deck. That was all he needed! More animals!

Chapter 2

Alvin was having a ball. There was so much a chipmunk could do on a cruise ship! He squirted sunscreen on the deck, and all the chipmunks slid across it—until Dave, carrying a tray of tropical drinks, accidentally slipped on it and wiped out.

Alvin sneaked up into the captain's bridge, the high-tech control room at the very top of the ship, and used the captain's microphone to make a very important announcement. He let all the passengers know that kids were allowed in the grown-ups' serenity pool. He managed to scurry away just as the captain burst into the room. Good thing he was small—and fast!

But at the waterslide Alvin discovered he was *too* small. The top of his furry head wasn't anywhere close to the line on the sign that said, YOU MUST BE THIS TALL. But that didn't stop Alvin for long. He grabbed a shoe, hopped onto it, and surfed down the waterslide anyway. Gnarly! Only Dave, hopping on one foot because he was missing a shoe, was waiting for him at the poolside. He was not happy. But he couldn't stop Alvin. Alvin used a line of fluttering flags across the deck as a zip line and sped away as Dave, swinging a pool net, tried to catch him.

As Dave pursued Alvin, the person dressed as a pelican appeared out of nowhere and put out a large webbed foot, blocking him.

And Alvin kept on running.

The chipmunk heard music, and Alvin could never resist a good song. He headed to the outdoor stage, and there, in front of the band shell by the pool, The Chipettes were singing one of their Top 40 hits. Swimmers in the water were bobbing their heads to the catchy tune, and Alvin hopped right across them, like they were stepping-stones. Alvin looked over his shoulder. Dave was still following him, and he was really mad. Alvin knew there was only one thing to do when he was in trouble—run! There was nowhere else to go. He had to jump onstage!

Brittany was annoyed as he began singing along with her. He was stealing her spotlight! The crowd went crazy. It was international singing sensation Alvin! They were clapping and cheering, and Alvin was bowing. He waved to the passengers and headed for the wings. Then he saw Dave there, waiting for him. Alvin turned right around and took a dive off the stage, into the arms of his enthusiastic fans.

"Al*vinnnn*!" screamed Dave. How was he going to tame this out-of-control chipmunk?

Chapter 3

Alvin was sitting on the edge of his bed in the cabin in his pajamas. Dave was lecturing him. Theodore and Simon were eavesdropping while they got ready for bed.

"We talked about setting rules, Alvin," said Dave sternly.

Alvin was pouting. "I didn't know one of the rules was 'no fun allowed.'"

"When are you going to stop acting like a child?"

"When are you going to stop treating me like a child?" Alvin snapped.

"I'll stop treating you like a child when you start acting like a grown-up!" Dave was yelling again.

"I'll start acting like a grown-up when you—" Alvin stopped as The Chipettes emerged from the bathroom, singing.

Dave sighed, frustrated. "Not now, girls!" He checked his watch. It was later than he'd thought. "I have to get ready for dinner with the captain," he said. He wasn't looking forward to apologizing for Alvin's antics.

"We're having dinner with the captain!" Brittany was excited.

"No, I am." Dave sighed. "All the chipmunks are staying here tonight." And with that announcement he went into the bathroom to get ready, shutting the door behind him.

Brittany plopped down beside Alvin. "This is so unfair!" She wanted to have fun on her vacation, too. She didn't want to be stuck inside the cabin all night. "It's not fair to us, it's not fair to Dave, and it's not fair to the captain, who I'm sure was really looking forward to dining with me." After all, she thought, how often did he get to entertain a real-live diva?

Simon approached Brittany. He hated to see

her so upset. "Why don't I speak with Dave? See if I can smooth things over."

Alvin shrugged his shoulders, skeptical that it would make any difference. He knew how Dave got when he was mad. All he seemed to care about was following the rules.

Simon knocked on the door to the bathroom and chirped as cheerfully as he could, "Knock, knock."

"What is it, Simon?" Dave sighed, opening the door. He was wearing a tuxedo and clearly struggling to knot his bow tie correctly. These cruise ship dinners were very fancy, much fancier than Dave was used to.

Simon whispered confidentially to Dave, "Well, I would never say this to Alvin—goodness knows he can be totally irresponsible—but I have a suggestion."

"You have a suggestion for *me*?"

"Alvin's been driving me crazy a lot longer than he's been driving you crazy," explained Simon.

Simon had a point. "All right, what is it?"

Simon cleared his throat. He was kind of an expert on Alvin. "Imagine Alvin is a spirited racehorse," he began.

"That's your advice?" Dave was not impressed.

"I'm not done yet, Dave," said Simon.

"Sorry. Alvin's a racehorse. . . ." He glanced in the bathroom mirror and tucked one end of the bow tie into the knot he'd made and watched it come undone. He could not remember how to tie it properly.

Simon leaped up to his shoulder and reached around, taking the two ends of the bow tie in his paws. As he expertly began passing one end over the other, he continued speaking. "And imagine you are his incredibly helpful jockey, who's there to guide him down the racetrack of life. But if you hold the reins too tight, that racehorse is going to fight and buck, which is no fun for anyone. On the other hand, if you loosen the reins just a little—"

"He'll run right off the track and crash into the fence," interrupted Dave.

"I know you want to protect Alvin," said Simon, "but sometimes kids will rise to the occasion if you just show them a little trust." He gave the bow tie a last pull.

Dave looked in the mirror. His tie was perfect. He was impressed. Maybe Simon had a point about Alvin after all. "Okay, guys," he said, coming back into the suite. "Room service is on its way. Lights out by nine o'clock."

Eleanor, startled, shared a look of surprise with Brittany and Jeanette. "Um, Dave, if we're going to be stuck in the room—"

"Because of Alvin!" interrupted Brittany, still furious.

Even Theodore chimed in. "Can we at least watch a movie?" His plump face was filled with disappointment.

"Well . . . sure, guys, let me see what's on," said Dave, and then he took a look at Simon's face. Maybe the chipmunks really were old enough to make some of their own decisions. His eyes met Alvin's. "You know what? Why don't you pick the movie?"

"You mean it, Dave?" Alvin brightened up at once.

"Absolutely." Dave glanced over at Simon, who gave him a big thumbs-up. The girls immediately began scrolling through movie titles on the television.

Dave took a last look at his tie in the mirror and headed to the door. He stopped when he noticed Theodore holding out something toward him in his little paws.

"Wait, Dave, before you go, I made something for you." He held up a necklace of twisted multicolor pipe cleaners and dried macaroni. Theodore was beaming with pride, but the necklace was hideous.

"Whoa! That's really . . ." Dave gulped, uncertain of what to say. It didn't really go with his tuxedo. "That's really nice of you."

Theodore blushed. "I made it soft so you can sleep in it, and I put all the colors in it, so it will go with everything! You never have to take it off!" He was still holding it out for Dave to take.

"I'll put it on as soon as I get back from dinner," said Dave, patting Theodore on the head.

"Or you could put it on now, so everyone at the captain's table can see it!" Theodore was looking at Dave with big, loving eyes.

Dave had no choice. He had to put on the necklace. Reluctantly, he took it from Theodore and dropped it around his neck. He knew he looked ridiculous, but if he had any last doubts, Alvin put them to rest.

"Nice. A real chick magnet," chuckled Alvin.

Theodore beamed with delight, not catching the sarcasm in Alvin's voice.

Dave took a deep breath. "All right, guys, have fun." And then he remembered that he was speaking to the chipmunks, and he caught himself. "But not too much fun, because I'm still very disappointed in you, Alvin."

Alvin nodded in agreement, very serious. But the moment the door was shut and he heard Dave's footsteps disappearing down the corridor, he gave a little wave to the door. "Good-bye, Dave," he whispered, and then he whirled around to face The Chipettes. "Hello, ladies!"

Alvin whipped off his pajamas, revealing beneath them a perfect white dinner jacket. Alvin was ready for action.

Chapter 4

Simon couldn't believe it; he was panic-stricken. What would Dave say? "Where are you going?"

Alvin rubbed his paws together, a gleam in his eyes. "The casino! I'm feeling lucky."

"Oh no. No, no, no. Dave said . . ." Simon was desperate. For all his talk of racehorses with Dave, he had no idea how to handle Alvin when he decided to take off.

"Dave said we were old enough to make our own decisions," said Alvin.

"He meant we were old enough to choose a movie!"

Alvin laughed as he looked at the television screen. "We're clearly not. Check out what Theodore just picked."

Theodore's little face fell. "What's wrong with this?" The opening credits had just started to roll across the screen, and Theodore couldn't wait to watch one of his favorite movies.

"It's for babies," sneered Alvin dismissively. "Which is why Dave treats us like babies. Munk up, Theodore." He grabbed the remote out of Theodore's hand and changed the movie. "There, that's better," he said with a smile. He tossed the remote onto the bed and headed for the door.

Simon sighed and took off down the narrow cruise ship corridor after Alvin. The girls looked at each other, pleased.

"Who's up for salsa night?" asked Brittany. "But what to wear . . . what to wear . . ." Dave and Alvin were dressed up, after all. The girls needed something fancy.

Eleanor jumped up onto the stateroom desk, her green eyes sparkling. "I know!" She reached into the welcome basket and poured a little tin of fruit candies out onto some sparkly fabric. It was time to party!

Chapter 5

The casino was hopping. The slot machines were spinning, dealers were passing out cards at lightning speed, and the dice were rolling. Alvin, standing on the edge of a green felt table, looked very suave in his dinner jacket. He was watching the dice carefully.

An attractive woman in a long gown and jewels threw a pair of dice, which landed right near Alvin. The dots on them added up to seven, and everybody cheered. The casino dealer pushed a large stack of chips over to the woman. Alvin had conveniently climbed on top. "We have a winner," Alvin said, winking at the woman. She laughed flirtatiously.

Simon, still wearing his pajamas, was looking all over the casino for Alvin. He scurried between tuxedo pants and the shimmery pleats of evening gowns, but he couldn't see over the heads of the people. Finally, he scrambled up on top of one of the slot machines and peered around. Nothing. Not a sign of Alvin anywhere! Using the slot machine handle as a springboard, he leaped onto the tray of a passing waitress. The slot machine's dials started spinning, lights started flashing, bells were ringing! The machine was spitting out hundreds of dollars in quarters! Simon was a winner. But he didn't know it. He had to find Alvin before he got into any trouble.

Meanwhile The Chipettes had taken over the dance floor. Not a lot of people could see them, but the girls were letting loose and having fun. Until Eleanor accidentally stepped on some lady's toe.

"Ow!" she screamed.

"Sorry!" squeaked Eleanor.

The young woman, with an attitude as big as her hair, looked down and saw a chipmunk dancing around by her ankles. "Ew!" she screamed again.

Was it a rat? But it was covered in sequins. And tiny fruit. And it was talking. "What are you?"

The woman's voice was loud, and everyone was listening. The music screeched to a halt.

"We are The Chipettes," said Brittany, posing. How could anyone not know who she was? She was on her way to the International Music Awards.

"I'm Eleanor!" said Eleanor, being friendly.

"And my sister was just trying to apologize," added Brittany, noticing how mad the young woman looked.

A friend of the young woman stepped forward. "What's she sorry for? Stepping on my friend's toe? Or for her busted, tired dance moves?"

Brittany didn't let anyone insult her sisters. "Oh no you didn't!"

The crowd leaned in, eager for a fight. Another girl, with long fake fingernails, stepped forward, egging them on. "Oh yes she did!" She wagged one of her fake fingernails in Brittany's face.

Brittany's paws were on her hips. "Get those press-on nails outta my face unless you wanna meet my claws." When she needed to, Brittany could get tough. She held up her claws at the woman. "And yeah, baby, they are *real*!"

"Oooh!" said the crowd.

"Oh, you wanna go?" said the young woman Eleanor had stepped on. She took off her hoop earrings and handed them to a friend.

The Chipettes were staring down the woman and her two friends, their paws on their hips.

Brittany snapped her fingers at the DJ. "Hit it!"

The music blasted through the speakers, and The Chipettes began strutting their stuff. They danced their hearts out, and the crowd was amazed. At first, the other women tried to keep up, but they knew they were no good. These Chipettes had star power!

From the blackjack table to the dance floor, the chipmunks had triumphed. By the end of the night, *everyone* was talking about them.

Chapter 6

Dave was squirming in his seat in the dining room. "Captain, I'm truly sorry about what happened. But Alvin—he's a kid, and he's just trying to have some fun." He smiled at the ship's captain, but the captain was not amused.

"There's nothing wrong with fun," said the captain, stone-faced. "Our pelican mascot makes sure everyone on our ship has fun. But my number-one priority is my passengers' safety. We simply cannot have Alvin put himself, or anyone else, at risk."

Dave nodded. "I understand."

"I'm afraid," added the captain, in an even more

serious tone, "that if Alvin breaks any more shipboard rules, I will be forced to make him walk the plank."

Dave looked taken aback. "I'm sorry, what?"

Without cracking even a hint of a smile, the captain explained, "That was a joke."

Dave wasn't so sure, but he tried to muster a weak laugh. "Oh. Yes. Very . . . funny."

"But in all seriousness," continued the captain (who seemed to be nothing but serious), "if Alvin violates any more of our rules, there will be consequences."

"Of course, Captain. Last thing we want is anyone getting hurt."

The waiter was about to pour pea soup into a bowl in front of Dave when the pelican guy bumped into him—and the soup went all over Dave's lap! Dave screamed and jumped up. The waiter, apologizing to both Dave and the captain, tried to wipe at Dave's pants, but Dave didn't pay him any attention. He'd noticed something about the pelican, who was hurrying away. Something familiar. He wasn't so sure that what had just happened was an accident. Excusing himself, he followed the guy out of the dining room and met up with him in the corridor.

"Do you have a problem with me?" Dave asked.

A voice, muffled behind the pelican mask, answered, "You bet I have a problem with you."

"Why?" Something about the way the guy waddled and the way he spoke reminded Dave of someone, but he couldn't think who it was.

"As if you don't know," sneered the pelican.

"I don't know," said Dave.

At that moment the pelican guy whipped off his bird mask and revealed the bald head of Ian Hawke. Ian Hawke—former CEO of Jett Records, former music producer, former manager of The Chipettes. Ian Hawke—the guy who would do anything to The Chipmunks to make himself famous. Ian Hawke—pelican guy.

"Ian? What . . . what are you doing here?"

"I'm working, Dave," said Ian sarcastically.

"This is your job?" Dave was confused. Ian was a wheeler-dealer. A big gun in the music industry. But apparently something had gone wrong.

"Yes!" said Ian bitterly. "There aren't too many record labels dying to hire the guy who blew it with The Chipmunks, blew it with The Chipettes, and passed on Justin Bieber. Twice."

"Ian, I'm sorry you lost your job and"—Dave caught a glance of the ridiculous pelican mask—"and your dignity. But spilling things, hot things, on me isn't going to bring any of that back."

Ian looked thoughtful, like he was really taking in what Dave was saying. "You're right, Dave. It is too late for me to get my old life back." He smiled brightly. "But it's not too late for me to ruin yours!"

"You want to ruin my life?"

Ian rubbed his pelican wings together. "Well, let's not get ahead of ourselves. How about we just start with your vacation? If I see The Chipmunks break so much as one rule, I'm going straight to Captain Correlli. You're in my house now!"

If he had been wearing a fancy suit and dark glasses, he might have seemed more menacing. As it was, he just looked like a pelican throwing a temper tantrum. Dave had to stifle his laughter.

Ian was clearly flustered. "I mean, technically it's not a house, it's a ship. And technically it's not really mine, it's owned by the cruise line. And technically I don't work for the cruise line but for a temp agency that provides costumed characters to cruise lines and auto shows and minor league ball games. But"—he stopped and pointed two fingers at the googly eyes on the pelican mask tucked under his arm and then at Dave's eyes— "I'll be watching you!"

And this time Dave really was worried. Ian was angry and a little crazy, and he clearly wanted revenge. Ian had tried to steal The Chipmunks from Dave once before, and he'd also tried to ruin their biggest concert, so he couldn't relax for a minute with Ian onboard. It was a good thing he'd made sure the chipmunks stayed safe in their room tonight. They were all going to have to be careful.

He opened the door to their cabin and saw little Theodore sitting on the edge of the bed staring at the television. He was chewing on his paws. And his fur was standing on end as if he'd placed his finger in an electric socket.

"Theodore?" said Dave quietly, concerned.

Theodore leaped up into the air like he'd been hit by lightning. "Please don't eat my brain!" he screamed.

Dave glanced at the screen and instantly recognized the movie. It was a grown-up horror movie filled with gore. He couldn't believe it! "What are you doing? That's *Jungle Monster Four*. Alvin, how could you let him watch this?"

He'd instinctively turned to Alvin's bed to yell at him, and it took him a moment to realize that no one was in it. It was empty. Alvin wasn't there. "Simon!" said Dave, whirling around in his fury. "How could you let Alvin sneak out?"

But Simon's bed was empty, too.

Frustrated, Dave turned to The Chipettes. "Girls, how could you let Simon . . ." But before he could finish, he realized that they were gone as well. All the chipmunks were gone except Theodore. It was beginning to sink in. They were in trouble. Now Dave looked like he'd been watching a horror movie. He noticed the sparkly fabric from the gift basket had three dress-pattern shapes cut out of it. "Oh no. No, no, no!"

Chapter 7

lvin and Tessa, the girl he'd met while playing dice, were now hanging out at the roulette wheel. He'd been letting her know that he was a pretty famous singer.

"Seriously? You're up for an International Music Award?" she asked, clearly impressed.

"Yup," bragged Alvin. "We fly there right after the cruise. Hoping to take home Record of the Year."

"Whoa! That would make you, like, the youngest winner ever!"

"I'm not *that* young," said Alvin, trying to act suave. "I mean, I'm hanging out in the casino *way* past my bedtime. Not that I have a bedtime. No one tells me what to do."

Unfortunately, he was interrupted by Dave running pell-mell into the casino and shouting at the top of his lungs, "Al*vinnnn!*"

Alvin froze. Gulped. Oh no. "Who's Alan?" he said to the girl. He was trying to act cool. "Anyway, love to chat more, but right now I gotta run." He took the girl's hand in his paw, gave it a quick kiss, and leaped away—but unfortunately he landed on the roulette wheel going round and round and round like an amusement park ride. He was stuck, running in place.

Dave grabbed him by the scruff of his neck. "You are in a lot of trouble, young man!"

Alvin glanced over at the girl, humiliated. He didn't look like a suave pop star anymore—just a naughty little chipmunk.

Dave, holding Alvin by the scruff of his neck, was storming through the casino when he passed by Simon—at the blackjack table. The little chipmunk was staring mesmerized at the cards in front of him.

"Simon?" Dave couldn't believe it. Simon had

disobeyed him, too!

"I wasn't betting, Dave, I swear!" exclaimed Simon when he saw him.

But at that exact moment one of the casino dealers slid a huge pile of money right in front of him. Simon had just won big. "Your winnings, sir," he announced.

"Awww, the new guys always win," said another gambler next to Simon.

Dave grabbed Simon and dragged him out of the casino—without his money. He was furious. He marched down the cruise ship hall with both of them in his arms.

"I didn't sneak out," protested Simon. "I mean, I did. But only to stop Alvin."

Once they got back to their cabin, he'd make Dave understand everything. Only it didn't look like that was going to happen. Because standing in front of the stateroom door was a giant pelican. And next to the pelican was the captain of the ship. And he was very angry.

Chapter 8

Alvin was defiant. The captain had given all the chipmunks a stern warning about what would happen if they got in trouble again. Alvin sat on his bed, mad. "So what's the captain gonna do?" he said to Dave. "Make us walk the plank?"

"There's a plank?" said Theodore, terrified.

"There's no plank!" yelled Dave, at his wits' end. "But if you disobey me one more time, you will be off the ship. And you will miss the International Music Awards. Do you understand?"

Eleanor, like Theodore, was near tears. "Yes, Dave."

"Uh-huh," said Jeanette, showing no emotion.

"Of course," chirped Brittany, rolling her eyes. "But if those girls challenge us to another dance-off, is it okay if we . . ." Dave was glaring at her. "No, of course not. Never mind."

Alvin was scratching his head, thinking. "Uh, Dave?" he said carefully.

Dave turned to him. He knew Alvin was the ringleader.

Alvin continued, "But what if we need to disobey you?"

"And why would you need to do that?"

"Well, let's say for instance that you tell me to stay put." He stood up and pretended to be Dave, making his voice lower. "*Alvin, if you move from that lounge chair, you're grounded!*"

All the other chipmunks had crowded around, listening.

"But then," continued Alvin, getting carried away, "I happen to see pirates climbing up ropes on the side of the ship. Now, it would be easy for me to take my pocketknife and cut the ropes. But I have to stay put. Or do I?"

Dave shook his head, not amused in the least.

"Yes, Alvin, you do. And what are you doing with a pocketknife?"

Alvin threw up his paws and assumed an expression of complete innocence. "What pocketknife?"

"Give it to me," said Dave sternly. He held out his hand. "You could cut yourself."

"So, I could have saved the whole ship from robbage and pilgering, and you'd still ground me?" asked Alvin, reluctant to turn over his pocketknife.

Simon sighed. "There's no such word as *robbage*, Alvin. And it's *pillaging*. But Alvin has a point, Dave. There must be times when you trust us to take matters into our own hands, even if you've told us otherwise. Surely you trust me."

Dave met Simon's eyes. "I trusted you tonight, and look where that got me!"

Simon hung his head in shame. Dave was right. He had messed up. Big-time. He'd have to show him that he was responsible. He needed to earn back Dave's trust.

But Alvin just wanted to find a way to keep on having fun.

Chapter 9

Dave was keeping a close eye on the chipmunks. It was daytime now, and Dave took them all up to the deck of the cruise ship together. The Chipmunks and Chipettes were back in their regular clothes, and Dave was in shorts and a T-shirt. Theodore's homemade pasta necklace was still draped around his neck. They were looking for something safe to do. The sun was shining on the waves. They were far out in the ocean, no land in sight.

"You're lucky Captain Correlli has allowed you one more activity," Dave said to Alvin.

"Hang gliding, Dave?" joked Alvin sarcastically.

And then he gasped when he saw where Dave had brought them.

They were at the shuffleboard court.

"Shuffleboard?" said Alvin in horror. Only old people played shuffleboard.

"By my calculations, it appears to be ten percent shuffle and ninety percent bored," added Simon.

Jeanette giggled. "That's funny!"

Simon blushed, flustered. He adjusted his glasses. "You . . . you . . . really think so?"

Jeanette giggled again and looked down awkwardly. Simon didn't know what to say. Jeanette was so pretty—the prettiest of The Chipettes, in his opinion.

Alvin was staring at the shuffleboard court. "You know, Dave, I think I'd prefer the plank."

"Sorry, Alvin, this is what you get to do. And now I get to do something I haven't done in a loooong time. Absolutely nothing."

Dave pulled up a lounge chair and laid down on it with a magazine. At last! Now he could enjoy a little bit of vacation himself. From time to time he glanced up at the chipmunks playing shuffleboard.

Brittany lined up a shot, and Alvin began whispering like a sports announcer at a golf tournament. "Brittany approaches her puck, adjusts her stance, looks over at me, annoyed, wondering if I'm ever going to shut up, realizes I'm not, and makes her move. . . ."

Brittany gave the puck a halfhearted push with her stick.

"Ooh! And it's short! A costly error that's going to haunt her the rest of her career," narrated Alvin.

Brittany was not amused. "You can make all the jokes you want, Alvin, but not even you can make this interesting."

There was nothing Alvin liked better than a challenge.

He looked around the deck of the ship at the sunbathing tourists. When he saw a kid holding the string of a kite, he got a mischievous look in his eyes. This could be a little more fun, he thought.

"Think I can't make this interesting?" Alvin challenged Brittany.

"What are you doing?" said Brittany. "Dave is watching us."

"Brittany, the poor guy hasn't had a moment's peace since he met us," whispered Alvin. "He's exhausted." His back to Dave, Alvin held up his fingers and began counting backward from five. "In three . . . two . . . one. . . ."

The magazine Dave had been reading slipped from his hands onto the deck. Dave's chin fell to his chest. Alvin didn't even need to turn around or wait for Dave to snore. He knew Dave was asleep. And Alvin was ready.

"Theodore, I'm going to need these doughnuts," he said, turning to Theodore, who was holding a plate of chocolate-covered doughnuts. "Time to turn punishment . . . into *fun*ishment." With a flick of his wrist, Alvin slid the plate of doughnuts along the deck so that they landed right at the feet of the kid flying the kite. The kid looked down at Alvin. Alvin raised a single eyebrow.

A moment later the boy was happily munching on Theodore's doughnuts—and Alvin had strapped himself into the kite like it was a parasail.

It was time to take off!

Alvin burst into song as he flew up into the sky!

Down below, the girls and Theodore were using all their strength to hold on to the string.

"C'mon, Simon, grab on," begged Theodore.

"Forget it. I am walking away from this one. All I ever do is try to save him, and it only gets me in trouble!" Simon stormed off.

Up in the cloudless blue sky Alvin was having the time of his life. He was flying! Far below him, he could see the tiny ship and the miniscule dots of color that were Brittany, Jeanette, Eleanor, and Theodore struggling to hold on to the string. The wind picked up, and Alvin soared even higher.

The kite string was dragging the chipmunks across the deck. It was lifting them into the air! They weren't big enough to keep it from flying away. As they took off into the air, Theodore reached out and grabbed one last doughnut.

At the very last minute, Simon glanced back and saw what was happening. Alvin was in trouble. Again. But what could Simon do?

He rushed over, grabbed the very end of the kite string, and managed to anchor it to the leg of Dave's lounge chair. Simon sighed with relief. They were safe.

"We're okay!" squealed a relieved Brittany.

"Sh!" whispered Simon, pointing at Dave. He was still asleep, and the last thing they needed was for him to wake up.

"We're okay!" whispered Brittany.

But they weren't.

A gust of wind blew up, and the lounge chair began sliding across the deck.

The kite flew even higher.

The kite string pulled the lounge chair across the shuffleboard court, wrapped around Simon's leg, and then broke as it hit the safety rail. The kite, with Alvin attached to it and five chipmunks clinging to its string, took off into the air.

"*Aaaaaa!*" screamed six little high-pitched voices.

But no one heard them. They were already too far away from the ship.

Chapter 10

Dave jolted awake. Where was he? Why was his deck chair slammed up against the railing? And where were the chipmunks? He whirled around, looking for them. They weren't by the shuffleboard court anymore. They weren't even on deck.

From far away up in the clouds, he heard the faintest high-pitched wail.

Dave shielded his eyes from the glare of the sun and looked up. Squinting, he could just make out six chipmunks attached to a kite disappearing beyond the horizon.

"No. No. *No!*"

Dave was frantic. He had to rescue them. At once. There wasn't even time to call for help. He scanned the cruise ship looking for a solution, and his eyes settled on a hang glider that was on display. He ran over to it and began releasing it from its security ropes.

"Hey!" Ian, still in his pelican suit, was right there. He took off the pelican mask and tucked it under his arm so that it was easier to talk. "You want to go hang gliding, you sign up at the excursions desk like everyone else."

"No, you don't understand. . . ." Dave looked up. By now the chipmunks were just a tiny speck in the distance.

"I think I do. Dave Seville is *soooo* special, the rules don't apply to him," said Ian sarcastically.

"That's not it, Ian," protested Dave. "You need to get the captain."

"I think he's going to agree with me on this one, Dave."

Dave wasn't listening. He was pushing the hang glider to the edge of the cruise ship.

"Hey, where do you think you're going?"

demanded Ian. He dropped the pelican head and pulled on Dave's arms.

"Let go!" screamed Dave.

"You let go!" screamed Ian.

Dave was holding on to the hang glider, and Ian was holding on to Dave, when a huge gust of wind swept the hang glider up into the air and far out across the surface of the water.

"Don't let go!" screamed Dave.

They crash-landed in the ocean. As they bobbed to the surface, the cruise ship sailed away.

Chapter 11

The chipmunks clung to Theodore's chocolate-covered doughnut like a life raft. The wind had finally died down, and the kite had dropped them somewhere in the middle of the vast, empty ocean.

"I don't think I can make it much longer," whimpered Theodore. "I'm so hungry."

No one said anything.

"Just one bite," he pleaded.

"No," said Simon.

"A nibble?"

"No nibbles," said Simon.

"Maybe I can just lick the glaze?" suggested Theodore.

Simon snapped. "The glaze is what's keeping us alive! Its high fat content is creating a waterproof barrier that should allow us to float for days."

"*Days?*" said Theodore, alarmed. "I'll starve to death."

"Actually," said Jeanette. "There are many other things that will kill you before starvation. Dehydration, sunstroke—"

A gasp from Brittany interrupted her. "An island!"

At first, Jeanette didn't realize what Brittany had said, and she continued her lecture on ocean survival. "Mmm, no . . . an island wouldn't kill us. In fact, it would probably be helpful. So if you see one, you should definitely say something."

Brittany rolled her eyes and pointed at a palm tree–studded island. "Um, Jeanette?"

"Oh!"

All the chipmunks, clinging to the doughnut, started paddling toward the white crescent of a tropical beach.

Eventually the waves washed them ashore.

"We're alive! We're alive!" squealed Eleanor,

grateful to feel the sand beneath her paws.

"Good," said Brittany with a little shake that sprayed water on everyone else. "Because now I'm going to kill Alvin!"

Brittany threw herself on Alvin like a wild animal—hitting, kicking, biting, and scratching. Simon tried to pull her off.

"C'mon, no one's killing anyone," he said to her. "No matter how much they deserve it." He glared at Alvin, who was still struggling to catch his breath.

"Thank you," said Alvin, straightening his shirt. He stepped into the middle of the group, ready to take charge as usual. "Look, guys, we've got nothing to worry about. Dave knows we're gone by now; he probably has the whole Coast Guard looking for us. Meantime, why don't you all just relax and have a bite of that doughnut. . . ."

Theodore was licking his fingers sheepishly. He had just popped the last of the chocolate-covered doughnut into his mouth. He had eaten the whole thing. It was a little salty from the ocean water, but still delicious.

"Oh," Theodore said, embarrassed. "Did you guys want some?"

They didn't have any other food. And who knew if there was food on the island? Or how long it would take for them to be rescued?

Of if they would ever be rescued at all?

Because despite Alvin's confidence, all the chipmunks knew that there was a good chance no one had seen them fly away—and no one knew where they were.

Chapter 12

Ian's pelican suit had filled with air, and it bobbed along the surface of the water like an inflatable life raft. Dave was clinging to it. Every few minutes Dave scanned the horizon, frantically looking for the chipmunks. The sun was lower in the sky. It would be night soon.

"Alvin! Simon! Theodore!" screamed Dave. His words drifted across the vast ocean and disappeared. "Can't you kick any faster?" he begged Ian.

"It's been two hours, Dave," whined Ian. "Thanks to thrice-weekly Pilates classes, I have legs that just won't quit, but they do slow down."

"Why don't you take off the webbed feet of

your costume, then, and let me use them? I'll kick better with them. They're like flippers."

"They don't come off," sneered Ian. "This is a complete suit. No quality mascot suit has removable feet."

"Then just take the suit off!"

"I can't," said Ian.

"Why not?"

Ian paused, embarrassed. "Because I'm not wearing anything underneath."

It was bad enough being lost at sea with Ian, but this was a little too much information for Dave. He felt seasick.

"Look!" shouted Ian.

"No, no, it's okay," said Dave at once. "I believe you."

"No, I mean, look!" Ian pointed a wing toward the horizon.

Dave saw the barest outline of a palm tree. Maybe the chipmunks had washed up there. He could only hope. He began kicking as hard as he could.

When they finally reached the beach, the sun was setting. There was no sign of the chipmunks, but Dave had seen a mountain and figured that if they climbed to the top of it, they'd be able to get a better view of the whole island. And maybe they'd find the chipmunks before nightfall.

Ian, dripping wet in his pelican costume, was rubbing together two sticks.

"What are you doing?" asked Dave.

"Making a fire. This can't be that hard."

"Forget the fire. We've got to start hiking."

"It's getting dark, Dave," complained Ian. "It's getting cold. We'll go in the morning."

"No, we'll go now," insisted Dave. He was worried about the chipmunks. They just had to be here.

"Jeez, Dave, are you always such a pain? No wonder those fur balls would rather fly off the ship than spend another day with you."

"They didn't do it on purpose. It was an accident. They're just kids." He stared off into the darkness of the trees, worried. "I don't know how long they can survive out there."

Chapter 13

On the other side of the island, six chipmunks were dragging their feet through the sand to make letters. They were sweating and exhausted, but they'd managed to write out *SOS!* But the letters weren't much bigger than they were. No one was going to see them from the sky. Only they didn't realize that.

"It won't be long before a rescue plane sees our message and gets us out of here," said Alvin, collapsing in the sand.

"I don't hear any planes," said Theodore. "Or helicopters. You think Dave is coming in a hot air balloon? 'Cause those things are really quiet."

"Theodore, it is highly unlikely Dave will be coming in a hot air balloon," said Simon, wiping sweat from his cheek with his shirt.

"But he is coming, right?" There was more than a little fear in Theodore's voice. The sun was going down, and soon it would start getting dark. He didn't like to be alone without a grown-up nearby.

"Of course he is," said Alvin reassuringly. "Just . . . maybe not today."

"Alvin's right. We should prepare to stay the night," said Simon.

Brittany was flabbergasted. "What? You guys expect me to sleep outside?" Her fur was already a mess from the perspiration. She needed a hot bath and a warm bed with clean sheets.

"Last I checked, Brit, we're chipmunks." Alvin laughed. "We're used to living in the wild."

Brittany tossed her head and made a small snorting noise. "No, we used to be used to living in the wild."

"C'mon, it's just one night," said Eleanor.

"One cold night," Brittany grumbled.

Alvin was not going to waste this opportunity to impress Brittany. It was time to show off. "We'll make a fire," he announced confidently. "We're always setting things on fire accidentally. How hard can it be when we put our minds to it?" He began gathering up stray pieces of driftwood washed ashore on the beach. "All I gotta do is light it."

Simon was standing back, shaking his head. "And how exactly are you intending to do that?"

"I will create a spark by striking this rock with my pocketknife," he explained. He'd seen it done on a television survival show. It didn't look that hard. He put his paw into his pocket, but it was empty. "The knife that Dave took from me."

Simon laughed at him.

"Oh, and I suppose you have a better idea, smart guy?"

"Actually, I do," said Simon. He took off his glasses and held the lenses toward the setting sun. "As you can see, the lens concentrates the energy of the sun, thus giving us *fire*!"

Simon couldn't believe it. He'd actually done it. He'd made fire! At his feet, sparks had begun to light. Simon had managed to set his own furry feet on fire! He frantically brushed the sparks off his paws, and they landed on the pile of driftwood that Alvin had collected. The pyre burst into flames.

"And that is how it's done," said Simon, pleased with himself.

Happily, the chipmunks huddled around their blazing fire, drying off and warming up.

"See?" said Alvin. "We're warm, and if a rescue helicopter comes by, they'll see us because of the fire! Everything's gonna be fine." He was always optimistic that things would turn out all right.

It grew darker, and the chipmunks grew sleepier.

"Good night, guys." Jeanette yawned.

"Good night," said Theodore. He picked up a handful of sand in each paw and threw it onto the fire. It went out. They were plunged into total darkness.

"Theodore!" yelled a chorus of little voices.

"What?" said Theodore, confused. "Dave always turns off the light after saying good night."

Simon groaned. "That fire was kind of keeping us warm."

"Can't you just relight it?" asked Theodore.

"How?" said Simon.

"With your glasses. And the sun!" explained Theodore. But the moment the words were out of his mouth, he realized his mistake. "Oh." There wasn't any sun anymore.

The chipmunks settled in for a long, cold night on their deserted island.

Chapter 14

The sun rose on six very hungry chipmunks. Alvin ripped some bark from a nearby tree and handed it out, humming an upbeat tune to lift everyone's spirits.

"And what is this supposed to be?" said a disgusted Brittany.

"Breakfast!" chirped Alvin.

"No, it's bark," corrected Brittany.

"For breakfast!"

"I can't eat bark," said Brittany, turning up her nose at it.

"Sure you can," said Jeanette in her soft voice. "I bet it's very good." She smiled sweetly at Alvin and took a tiny nibble from the bark he'd given her. Immediately she spit it out. "No it's not!"

"It's been eighteen hours since our last all-you-can-eat buffet on the cruise ship," Simon pointed out. "Perhaps it's time we got off this beach and started looking for food."

They shook the sand out of their fur and, with Alvin leading the way, headed into the dense jungle. Strange birds called out. Tangled vines caught at their feet. The sun barely shone through the thick fronds of the trees.

"If I know my horticulture—and I do," said Simon smugly, "this is a grove of mango trees."

"Then where are all the mangoes?" asked Alvin, looking around.

"Maybe Jungle Monster Four ate them all!" Theodore was trembling.

"Monsters aren't real," said Simon. "They're like the tooth fairy."

Theodore gasped, horrified.

Simon instantly realized his mistake and hurried to explain himself. "Except the tooth fairy is very real, and jungle monsters are not."

Meanwhile Alvin had scampered up a nearby tree, raced along one of its branches, reached the very end of it, parted the leaves, and revealed a giant mango.

Alvin, his nose twitching, inhaled its sweet aroma. He had opened his mouth to take an enormous bite when Brittany scurried up the tree and sat down right beside him. "You were planning on sharing that, right?" she said, one eyebrow raised.

Alvin was busted. "Of course," he lied.

"Oh, good. 'Cause it looked like you were going to eat it all by yourself."

"I would never do that," said Alvin with mock seriousness.

"I don't believe you!" chirped Brittany. And she snatched the mango out of Alvin's hands and skipped across the branches to another tree.

"Hey!" yelled Alvin.

The race was on!

Alvin leaped after her, and the two chipmunks began chasing each other, swinging from vines, up and down tree trunks and across leafy branches.

The mango in her paws, Brittany looked over her shoulder. Where was Alvin? She'd lost him! Suddenly, Alvin appeared out of nowhere and took a flying leap to a branch above Brittany. He grabbed the mango with his feet and dismounted the branch, landing on the ground like an Olympic gymnast. He twirled the mango with his paws like a basketball.

"Sorry, but I'm going to take my talents to South Beach," he taunted Brittany.

He had begun to scurry away when a giant stick shot out of the underbrush, tripping him up and sending the mango flying. Brittany tossed the stick aside, snatched the precious fruit out of the air before it landed, and took off triumphantly through the jungle.

But Alvin didn't give up that easily!

Appearing like Tarzan on a vine, he swung by Brittany and swiped the mango out of her hands. "I'll make sure to save you the pit!" he yelled as he made his getaway.

Brittany swung after him in hot pursuit, trying to avoid the obstacle course of trees growing close together. She was just about to catch up to him when her vine looped over a branch and caught her. Alvin was sure of his victory! He looked back at her in triumph . . . and smashed right into the trunk of a tree. The mango flew out of his hands yet again.

And this time it landed right at the feet of Theodore. He was stunned.

"Way to go, Theodore!" said Alvin "C'mon, we'll split it!"

"Don't listen to him," said Brittany. "He's gonna eat it all by himself. I'll share it with you." She fluttered her eyelashes at Theodore.

"Yeah, right! She's trying to trick you," said Alvin.

"No, you're trying to trick him," said Brittany.

"No, *you're* trying to trick him by saying I'm trying to trick him," said Alvin.

Theodore looked at Alvin. He looked at Brittany.

"He's lying, Theodore," said Brittany.

Theodore took a deep breath, held on to the mango for dear life, and ran! When it came to

The Chipmunks and The Chipettes are going to enjoy a vacation together—at sea!

While Dave relaxes,

Alvin and the gang take advantage
of all the cruise ship has to offer.

After they're sent to their
cabin for getting in trouble,
The Chipettes and The Chipmunks
try to entertain themselves,

but Alvin is super bored and has other ideas.

But his big ideas get the 'munks
into big trouble!

Who will come to the rescue?

Will Dave and Ian save the day?

food, nothing stopped this little butterball.

Brittany and Alvin couldn't believe it, though. They chased after him, scratching and clawing at each other in their rush to get close. Theodore ran as fast as his chubby legs could carry him. He ran and ran and ran through the jungle until a vine, stretched like a wire across his path, caught his foot.

Wipeout!

"Theodore, I am so sorry," said Jeanette seriously. She let go of the vine and grabbed the mango, which had fallen out of Theodore's hands.

With a quick toss, Jeanette threw the mango to Eleanor, who was ready to catch it. Except Eleanor wasn't a very good catcher, and the mango went sailing over her head.

All the chipmunks dived for it.

Paws wrestled and scrambled, and at last Jeanette emerged from the scuffle with the mango held high over her head. "Stop it! Stop it! Stop it!" she yelled at the others. "Look at us. One day on this island, and we've become . . . *animals*!"

But the other chipmunks weren't listening to her; they were frozen in place with terror. They had just heard twigs snapping and leaves rustling. A strange noise was coming from the jungle. It was coming to get them.

"What was that?" said Brittany, terrified.

"Jungle Monster!" Theodore said with a shudder.

The terrified chipmunks quickly assembled a makeshift catapult out of a vine and loaded it with the mango.

The bushes in front of them parted.

All the chipmunks screamed at the top of their lungs. Alvin launched the mango.

Splat!

The mango slammed into the face of the monster with a sickening thud.

"*Ow!*" cried the monster.

Chapter 15

Theodore was hiding his eyes, terrified. "Please don't eat us, Mr. Jungle Monster," he begged.

Only the monster wasn't a monster. It was a girl. And she was rubbing her head. "Uh, the name's Zoe, and I'm not a monster. I'm just a girl—" and she stopped midsentence and stared at the chipmunks. All of a sudden she realized she was talking to six small, furry animals. "A girl who's been on this island so long that I'm now imagining squirrels can talk," she said to herself.

Simon looked offended. "We're chipmunks!"

"Alvin and The Chipmunks," said Alvin proudly.

Zoe was rubbing her eyes and shaking her head like she was trying to get out something that was stuck in her ears. "Who?"

Brittany did a little dance move and fluttered her eyelashes. "I'm sure you've heard of The Chipettes. We're kind of world famous. Maybe this will help." She started singing.

Eleanor and Jeanette immediately started singing backup and dancing. Alvin couldn't resist; he joined in, too. In an instant, all the chipmunks were performing together.

But Zoe just looked confused. "Okay, okay, I'm gonna stop you right there. No idea what you are talking about."

The chipmunks were chattering; they couldn't believe it. Brittany was stunned. "Um, exactly how long have you been on this island?"

Zoe scrunched up her face, thinking. "Hmm. Let's see. I remember I got here on a Monday, so . . ." She was counting on her fingers. "Eight? Nine years?"

"Nine years?" gasped Simon. "You've been here nine years?"

"Or eight," answered Zoe. "But it was definitely on a Monday."

Brittany looked around at the overgrown jungle and remembered sleeping in the sand the night before. She couldn't do that again. "Guys," she said anxiously. "What if we're here nine years? What if we're here forever?"

But Alvin refused to give up hope. "I told you. Dave's coming."

Zoe's face brightened for a moment at the mention of Dave. "I used to think Dave was coming," she said.

The chipmunks' eyes widened.

"Dave Henderson," explained Zoe. "My supervisor at UPS. I used to fly cargo planes for them until the day I crash-landed in the ocean. And that day was . . . a Tuesday. Forget anything I said about Monday."

"But our Dave won't rest until he finds us. I'm sure of it. Right, Alvin?" said Theodore.

Alvin didn't look so sure, but he pretended to be confident to reassure Theodore. "Absolutely."

Simon shook his head. He wasn't buying it. He

knew they were in trouble. A lot of trouble.

But the person who really believed Alvin was Zoe. "Oh, man! I'm finally getting out of here? Wait till I tell the others!" she exclaimed with joy.

"There are others?" asked Jeanette, looking around. She didn't see anyone else in the underbrush.

"Can you imagine being stuck here all these years without anyone to talk to?" laughed Zoe, a little hysterically. "I'd lose my mind!" She looked like she already had.

A moment later Zoe led the chipmunks to an opening in the jungle, and there, arranged in a line, were five balls: a basketball, a golf ball, a baseball, a tennis ball, and a football. Each ball had a face and a name Zoe had given it.

The chipmunks didn't know what to say. They were kind of beginning to wish Zoe had been a jungle monster. That might have been less weird.

Zoe didn't notice, however, how uncomfortable they were. She was going on and on about her friends. "They survived the crash with me," she explained.

Still uncertain what to do, each of the

chipmunks went up to the balls and introduced themselves, pretending to make polite chatter. Zoe was telling the balls that Dave was coming to rescue them. She looked more wild-eyed than ever.

"Not Dave Henderson," she said, speaking to the tennis ball, "a different Dave. Can you believe it? We're finally getting off this island! This totally calls for a party. You guys hungry?"

The chipmunks weren't sure if she was still talking to the balls.

"I'm talking to you," Zoe said to the chipmunks.

Their faces instantly lit up with excitement. They were very hungry!

"Yeah!" said Theodore at once.

"You bet," said Jeanette.

"Yes!" said all the others.

"All right, let's go back to my place," said Zoe cheerfully.

"Is it far?" sighed Brittany. "Because I don't think I could walk another step."

"Who said anything about walking?" Zoe pulled back some branches and revealed a long zip line stretching far into the jungle.

Wow! thought Alvin. That looks like fun!

A moment later Zoe had taken off, with Alvin zooming right behind her high over the jungle valley. All the others followed, each one a little more terrified, with Theodore and Jeanette each clinging to the zip line for dear life.

The zip line went over the tops of the palm trees and finally ended outside a ramshackle hut deep in the jungle, surrounded by fruit trees. As each of the chipmunks came in for a landing, Zoe retrieved her ball friends from a basket she'd attached to the zip line.

"Wasn't that awesome?" said Zoe when most of the chipmunks had arrived.

Simon looked like he was about to be sick. "No, that wasn't awesome. It's a miracle we got here safely. In fact, the odds of a chipmunk getting hurt on a zip line are one out of six."

Eleanor crash-landed, tumbling to the ground.

Simon sighed. "Why do I always have to be right?"

All the chipmunks crowded around Eleanor,

who was holding her ankle. "I think I sprained it," she moaned.

"Awww, sweetie, we should get some ice on that right away," said Zoe helpfully. Only she didn't move. "Oh!" she said as the chipmunks stared at her. "I don't have any. I thought you might."

"No, we don't have any ice," fumed Simon impatiently. "Just like we don't have any shelter. Or any food."

"Bummer," said Zoe, disappointed. "Hey, you guys like bungee jumping?"

"Yes!" exclaimed Alvin instantly.

"*No!*" said Simon at the exact same moment. "Maybe you should just leave us alone so we can focus more on surviving and less on killing ourselves."

Zoe stepped back. "Man, that's a lot of uptight in such a little package!"

"I'm not uptight," yelled Simon, even angrier. "I just don't want to see anyone else getting hurt. Ow!" He grabbed his arm in pain, like he'd been stabbed by an invisible sword.

"What was that?"

Zoe looked around and saw a large, hairy spider scurrying away into the brush. She pointed at it. "Just a spider. They're all over the place."

A look of horror spread across Simon's face. He knew what kind of spider that was. He'd read about them. "That's a *Phoneutria bahiensis*! Its bite contains a neurotoxin!"

"So?" said Alvin.

"Alvin, *toxin* means 'poison.' And *neuro* means 'brain,'" explained Simon carefully, still clutching the bite on his arm, which was hurting more and more. He could feel the poison spreading through his body. To his brain.

"Oh. That's not good," said Alvin, genuinely concerned.

Simon began reciting the symptoms of the spider's bite like he was reading from a book. "Side effects include changes in personality, loss of inhibition, dry mouth—"

"Nah, I don't buy it," interrupted Zoe, who didn't look worried at all. "I get chomped on by one of those hairy fellas at least once a day, and I've never been affected. Right, Dunlop?"

She held up the tennis ball, which she made nod back to her in agreement.

The chipmunks exchanged worried glances.

They were on a deserted island. They were hungry. Eleanor had a sprained ankle. Simon had just been bitten by a poisonous spider. And the only person who might possibly help them was carrying on a conversation with a tennis ball!

Chapter 16

Dave and Ian were hiking up the rocky part of the mountain at the center of the island. It was tough going. And hot.

Ian was calling for the chipmunks. "Alvin? Simon? . . . Chubby one? Girl chubby one? Brittany? Jeanette?"

Dave stopped to wipe the sweat off his forehead and look around. "Ian, I know we've had our differences in the past, but I'm glad you can put all that aside to help me find them. I just hope they're okay."

"Who cares if they're okay? I just need them to be here. Let me break this down for you, Dave.

Record execs? They're a bunch of bloodsucking leeches—I should know, I used to be one. They'll spare no expense to find The Chipmunks. But if it's just you and me on this island? We're dead men."

Dave shook his head. "And here I am, thinking you've changed and don't only care about yourself."

Ian laughed bitterly. "Oh no, I assure you, Dave. Underneath this slowly disintegrating costume is the same ol' Ian Hawke. And it's a good thing, too. 'Cause at this point, my rage toward you and The Chipmunks is the only thing keeping me going." He paused and seemed more upbeat. "Shall we keep going?"

"Absolutely!" agreed Dave. "Why don't you keep an eye out for something to eat or drink, all right?"

"All right," agreed Ian, and then he paused, his eyes falling on the pasta necklace still hanging around Dave's neck. "Wait, right there!"

Dave looked around with no idea what Ian was talking about. "Where?"

"Around your neck," said Ian. He reached out for the pipe-cleaner-and-macaroni necklace. A little old pasta looked pretty good right now.

But Dave jumped back before Ian could grab it. "You can't eat this!" said Dave, alarmed. "It was a gift from Theodore."

"Oh, that makes sense," said Ian without cracking a smile. "'Cause it's really ugly."

"It's not ugly. It goes with everything, and it's soft enough to sleep in," insisted Dave. He reached up protectively to hold on to the necklace.

"And edible!" Ian lunged toward the necklace again, his mouth open.

"You will not eat my son's necklace!" screamed Dave.

Ian stopped. He took a step back. He peered at Dave. "He's not your son, Dave. He's just a chipmunk."

Dave was outraged. Theodore was not "just a chipmunk" to him.

"And by the way"—Ian laughed menacingly—"finding him and finding something to eat are not mutually exclusive."

And with those threatening words, he took off up the mountain.

Chapter 17

Another day had passed. As the stars came out over the vast sea and the tiny island, six little chipmunks curled up in the sand for another night lost and alone. The flames of a campfire flickered. Eleanor, her ankle splinted with sticks and seaweed, slept peacefully. But Alvin couldn't drift off. He was getting worried. Simon was tossing and turning like he was having a nightmare. Quietly, Alvin climbed up a tree and looked out to sea. "Where are you, Dave?" he whispered.

How could he know that not far from where he was, Dave, too, was worried? Dave sat on the edge of a cliff, wondering where his chipmunks might be. Were they even on the island? Were they even still alive?

And hidden away in her grass hut, Zoe couldn't sleep. She'd tucked her various balls into bed and she was trying to reassure them. And herself. "C'mon, guys," she muttered. "Quit being paranoid. They're not here to steal our . . ." Zoe glanced around nervously, making sure no one was listening, and then continued speaking in an even softer voice. "They're not here to steal our stuff. They don't even know it exists. And it's going to stay that way, as long as we all keep our mouths shut. You think you can do that?"

She looked sternly at the basketball and the golf ball and the baseball and the tennis ball and the football.

Not one of them said a word.

Chapter 18

Simon was the first one to wake up. His eyes popped open at dawn, and the first thing he did was rip the seaweed bandage off his arm. He tied the fronds of seaweed around his head like a bandanna and started to swagger off into the jungle.

Rubbing the sand out of his eyes, Theodore watched him leaving. "Simon? Where are you going?"

The early wind blew the seaweed bandanna around Simon's head. He looked like a pirate. And when he started speaking he had, strangely, a French accent. "Who is this Simon you speak of?"

"Um . . . you," said Theodore, confused.

"No. My name is not Simon. It is"—he paused for effect—"Simone."

Theodore blinked, even more confused. "That's pretty close to Simon."

"And yet completely different," said Simon (or Simone), twirling his whiskers. "Would you care to join me on my adventure?"

"What adventure?" asked Theodore timidly.

"The adventure called *life*!" exclaimed Simon with great joy.

Simon wasn't acting like himself. Still, Theodore knew he could trust him to make good decisions. Simon never got into trouble. "Okay," he agreed, and he scampered off into the jungle after Simon.

When Brittany awoke, they were nowhere in sight. She immediately started shaking Alvin. "Alvin, Alvin!"

"What, what is it?" Alvin was still sleepy.

"Simon and Theodore are gone," she said.

"They probably just went to get stuff for a shelter," said Alvin, his eyes shutting again. "It's all Simon can talk about."

Brittany shook her head. She was worried. "Still, it's not like either of them to wander off like that. Could you please go look for them?"

"Why can't you?" Alvin yawned and stretched.

"I have a situation of my own to deal with, Alvin!" yelled Brittany.

"Oh, right," Alvin apologized. "How's Eleanor doing?"

Brittany clicked her tongue against the roof of her mouth in disgust. "Eleanor's fine, but I'm talking about *me*. It's been two days since my last bath; I'm a mess! I can't get rescued looking like this!"

Alvin rolled his eyes, but he got up anyway and headed into the jungle to look for Simon and Theodore. "Simon? Theo?" he called.

And then he saw Simon. Right in front of him. Hanging upside down.

"*Bonjour*, my friend," said Simon, greeting Alvin in a mixture of French and English. He bounced out of sight and reappeared a moment later, still upside down.

"Simon? Are you . . . bungee jumping?" Alvin couldn't believe it.

"His name isn't Simon," said Theodore, coming up beside Alvin.

"It's Simone!" exclaimed Simon, bouncing into view again.

"Uh, that's pretty close to Simon," noted Alvin.

"I thought so, too!" agreed Theodore. "But he's acting totally different."

Then it hit Alvin what was going on. It was like Simon had undergone a complete change of personality. He didn't seem to have any more inhibitions. "It's the spider bite!" said Alvin. "Remember the side effects?"

"I remember none of this. Who are you?" Simon disappeared again.

Oh boy. This was worse than Alvin could ever have imagined. "Alvin," he said.

"Simone is pretty cool," said Theodore.

"It's Simon," corrected Alvin. "And no, he's not."

"Would you excuse us, Alvin?" Simon had bounced back again, grabbed Theodore, and sprung up into the air with him onto a high branch. Zoe was already up there. "Monsieur Theodore, it is your turn!" Simon began unfastening himself from the bungee cord.

"I've never done anything like this," Theodore squealed as Simon tied him onto the cord.

Alvin chased after him. "And you never will!"

"How can you let them do this? What are you thinking?" Alvin yelled at Zoe. After all, she might be weird, but Zoe was still a grown-up.

"I'm thinking, when did my dad wash up on this island?" answered Zoe, irritated. "We're having a good time here, and you gotta show up and be all uptight."

"Me? Uptight?" Alvin was stunned. "I'm not the uptight one. I'm the fun one! The cool one. Ask anybody!"

Theodore had wrapped the bungee cord around his tummy. He was getting ready to jump.

"Theodore!" shouted Alvin, stomping his foot. "You can't bungee jump. You get scared just watching a movie."

"Munk up, Alvin!" said Theodore. He leaped off the branch, screaming with joy all the way down.

Alvin couldn't believe it. What was going on? Wasn't anyone in charge anymore?

Chapter 19

Back at the camp, Jeanette had made her sisters beautiful dresses out of flowers.

Brittany was very pleased with hers. "Much better. Jeanette, these dresses are totally *adorbs*. I die."

Jeanette blushed, pleased. "Thank you. Oh, that reminds me! I also made these for you, Eleanor." She handed Eleanor a pair of bamboo crutches.

Eleanor wobbled around, getting the hang of them. "I had no idea you were so handy. I always thought that was me."

Jeanette was bursting with pride and now

revealed an impressive bamboo wheelchair. "And in case you get tired, I also made you this!"

Eleanor couldn't believe it. Now she felt really useless. "Oh, super," she said, trying to smile.

Meanwhile, Brittany wanted a bath. She found a small, rocky pool. When she dipped her paw into it, she was surprised that the water was perfectly hot, like it had come out of the tap. Steam rose from its surface. What she would have seen, if she'd been in an airplane, was that steam and smoke were also coming out of the large mountain looming over the island. But Brittany never imagined that her hot spring came from a volcano. She settled into her bath. "Ahh!"

Later on, Alvin returned to camp looking glum. "Hey," he said to the girls before plopping down in the sand.

Brittany was out of the bath now and brushing her hair with a comb made out of a shell. "Did you find Theodore and Simon?"

Alvin shook his head. "No, but I found Theodore and Simone."

"Who's Simone?" asked Jeanette, coming over.

At that moment, Simon swung into camp on a vine like he was Tarzan or Robin Hood or a movie pirate. The girls were really surprised. He bowed over Brittany's paw, took it in his, and kissed it. "*Enchanté*," he whispered in a deep voice.

Brittany giggled. "What's gotten into him?"

"Spider venom," said Alvin, unimpressed. "He thinks he's some sort of fun-loving French dude."

When Simon met Jeanette's eyes, he was speechless. He had never seen anything so beautiful before. He kissed her hand, and she blushed. "Oh!"

Distant thunder rumbled. Alvin looked up and noticed heavy rain clouds. "Hey Simon," he said.

Simon didn't even turn his head.

"Simone?" said Alvin, and that got Simon's attention. "I think we should get to work on a shelter."

"*Pourquoi?*" said Simone in French. And then in English he added, "Why? I can't imagine a better roof over our heads than the sky."

"I don't know, what about the kind of roof over our heads that's actually a roof? It's going to rain," said Alvin, irritated.

"What's a little rain? We cherish the water, for it is the water that nurtures the flower." Simon plucked a flower from a nearby bush, inhaled its scent, and then tucked it behind Jeanette's ear. She blushed.

Alvin was fed up. "Okay, this is crazy. Building a shelter was *your* idea. Yours. Not mine. Yours!"

The first drops of rain began to fall, and within a minute it had become a downpour. Alvin was running around gathering palm fronds to make a hut. "C'mon, everyone help me!"

Jeanette grabbed a rock and tried to hammer a palm frond into the ground. It didn't work.

"May I?" offered Simon, holding out his hand and smiling at Jeanette.

Jeanette gratefully handed Simon the rock. Surprisingly, he tossed it aside.

"What are you doing?" asked Jeanette.

Simon fixed Jeanette with a romantic gaze. "What I've wanted to do from the moment I laid eyes on you!" He took her by the hand and swooped her off to a nearby clearing to dance.

Who was this chipmunk? It certainly wasn't

serious Simon! He twirled Jeanette in his arms and expertly waltzed her around the clearing. Jeanette was entranced—especially when he began singing to her, too!

Alvin couldn't take it anymore. "This is nuts," he said to no one in particular. "They're going to catch pneumonia dancing in the rain like that." Wasn't anyone else worried?

"Is it raining? I hadn't noticed," gushed Jeanette as she glided by in Simon's arms. He was still crooning to her.

Alvin yelled at him, "You might want to save your voice in case we see a helicopter and have to scream for help!"

Eleanor was watching them, and she was jealous. She wished she could dance. She swayed back and forth on her crutches. "I think it looks like fun."

Simon overheard this, waved Theodore over, and, without ever stopping dancing, whispered something to him.

Biting his paws with nervousness, Theodore approached Eleanor. "Um, Eleanor? Would you care to dance?" he said, sheepishly.

"I'd love to!" responded Eleanor at once.

Theodore bit his lip, still unsure. "With me?"

"Yes, Theodore. But I . . ." She pointed to her bandaged ankle.

Theodore, suddenly inspired, literally swept Eleanor off her feet and danced her around in the rain.

But Alvin wasn't having any fun. "This is ridiculous! Do you know how slippery that dirt is? Last thing we need is someone else getting hurt."

Brittany was standing beside him, her arms crossed, furious. "I can't believe Jeanette's getting all the attention! I mean, I'm the pretty one! That's the way it's always been. I'm the pretty one, Jeanette's the smart one. You don't see me running around trying to be smart, do you? We should just stick to what we know."

"Yeah," agreed Alvin. "I'm the fun one, you're the pretty one."

"Yeah!" said Brittany. Just then a kick of Jeanette's sent a clump of mud flying right into Brittany's hair.

Alvin shouted to be heard above the rain and the singing. "You know, you ought to be careful kicking mud around like that. Someone could lose an eye!"

But no one was listening to him.

Alvin lost it. "Si*monnnn*!" he yelled at the top of his lungs.

Brittany was startled. She cleared her throat, knowing already that Alvin wouldn't like what she was going to say. But someone had to say it. And it might as well be her. "Alvin? You're starting to sound like Dave."

Alvin froze. His eyes widened. His mouth opened in a scream of horror. And a bolt of lightning lit up the sky.

Across the island, Dave woke up. He'd heard something. It was probably just thunder, but he ·could have sworn he'd heard Alvin's voice. He must have been dreaming. He lay back down and closed his eyes. Ian was watching him, and the moment he thought Dave was asleep again, he reached over and tried to take a bite of the macaroni necklace. But Dave swatted him away. It didn't matter how hungry they got—he was never taking off his present from Theodore.

Chapter 20

Alvin walked along the beach, gathering pieces of driftwood that the storm had washed ashore during the night.

"What are you doing?" asked Brittany, watching.

"Building a shelter," said Alvin, continuing to work. "Since I'm not the fun one anymore, I figure I may as well be the responsible one." He shuddered. He didn't want to be responsible, but someone had to do it. And with Simon turned into Simone and Dave gone, there was no one else.

"Ew. Really?" questioned Brittany. She thought for a moment. "Well, since I'm not the pretty one anymore, maybe I should build a shelter, too."

"Yeah, good luck with that," said Alvin wearily.

"You don't think I can do it?"

"I didn't say that. I thought it," Alvin admitted. "But I didn't say it."

While Alvin and Brittany worked in the hot sun, Zoe led the rest of the chipmunks through the jungle. Theodore and Eleanor sat on her shoulder, and Simon leaped over boulders and swung from tree branches. He was showing off for Jeanette. And Jeanette was impressed.

Sometimes he'd pick a piece of fruit and hand it to her.

At one point they came to a deep gorge, and the only way to the other side was to walk across a rotted-out log. Fearlessly, Zoe stepped onto it. On her shoulder Theodore trembled and grabbed Eleanor's hand out of fear. But they made it across safely.

Then it was Jeanette's turn. She hesitated. It was a long way down. Hundreds of feet. And at the bottom of the gorge were rapids. She wasn't sure she could do it—until Simon jumped ahead of her, turned around, and began walking backward across the log with his hands held out to her. Jeanette was frozen with fear. Simon gently lifted her chin so that she was looking right into his eyes and smiled at her reassuringly. Jeanette smiled back. She took a step. And then another. Step by step, never losing eye contact, Simon led her across the gorge.

And it was worth it.

Because on the other side was the most fantastic waterfall any of them had ever seen. The sun shone through sprays of crystal-clear water, creating two beautiful tropical rainbows.

"Whoa," exclaimed Zoe in an awed voice. "It's a double rainbow all the way! Whoa. . . . What does it mean?"

Chapter 21

Dave was exhausted. He took a sip from a muddy stream and sighed.

"What is it now?" asked Ian.

"Nothing," answered Dave. "I'm just worried about the chipmunks."

"Still?" said Ian, disgusted.

"Yes, still! They're still lost and I'm still worried about them."

"I don't know why you're so worried," said Ian. "I mean, alive they're superstars. Dead . . . they're legends!" He grinned. "We're talking back-catalog sales, tribute albums, pay-per-view funeral. . . ."

Dave looked horrified. "Hold it right there. You actually think I'm in this for the money?"

"If you're in it to meet women, you're doing a lousy job."

"I'm doing this because I love them, okay? And if something happened to them, I don't know what I'd do. Fine, go ahead, make fun of me."

Ian was staring at him, a smug smile on his face. "I can't. What could I possibly say that would make you feel stupider than you already are? You want to spend the rest of your life chasing after a bunch of spoiled brats, that's up to you."

Dave exploded. "They're not brats!"

"Really?" sneered Ian. "Not even Alvin?"

"You never bothered to get to know them. I mean, sure, Alvin can be kind of a handful, but he means well, he really does. He's just sometimes a little irresponsible, that's all. But c'mon: Simon? He's probably the most levelheaded kid I know. If anything, he's a little too uptight."

Dave could never have imagined that at that exact moment Simon was swinging from vines into a waterfall while Alvin was working in the hot sun to build a shelter for his friends. Things had really changed.

"And then there's Theodore. . . ."

Ian could barely contain his boredom. "Dave, I didn't care what you had to say about the first two. I can't imagine the chubby one is going to be any more interesting."

"You know what? Never mind," said Dave. "Let's get going."

"Now hold on, Dave. I do have one question."

"What?"

Ian looked thoughtful. At last, he said, "How do you spank them?"

Dave blew up. "*What?*" he screamed.

"I mean, what do you do?" Ian taunted him. "Lift up their tails or something?"

"I don't spank them!" said Dave forcefully. Even the idea of it was upsetting to him.

"Oh, okay. Sorry." Ian smirked. A wicked smile passed across his face. "Not even Alvin?"

"No!" yelled Dave. And he stormed off into the jungle with Ian following him.

Chapter 22

Simon dived into the pool beneath the waterfall. His enormous chipmunk cheeks were filled with air, and he was able to swim deep underwater. When he surfaced, he was actually in the space between the waterfall and the cliff. Behind him the water rushed down like a moving wall. In front of him a large pile of rocks blocked what looked like the entrance to a cave. Simon was curious. He pulled himself out of the water and managed to squeeze his tiny body between the cracks. He was ready to explore!

The walls of the cave gave off a pale green glow from a special kind of algae. It was magical. And even more magical was what Simon saw in the pale light. His eyes went wide. He couldn't believe it! He couldn't wait to surprise Jeanette with what he'd found.

Beside the pool the other chipmunks were getting worried. Simon had been underwater for a long time.

"He should have come up by now," Eleanor fretted.

"Maybe he hit his head on a rock and doesn't remember who he is!" said Theodore, panicked. He called out, "Simon, where are you?"

"Zoe, you gotta do something!" begged Jeanette.

"Okay, okay!" said Zoe, lazily getting up. She pulled the golf ball out of her pocket. "Callaway, find him and bring him back!" Zoe flung the ball right into the waterfall.

The chipmunks exchanged anxious glances. "You're kidding, right?" muttered Jeanette.

"If Callaway can't find him, no one can," said Zoe confidently.

And somehow she was right. A second later, Callaway flew right back to Zoe, who caught him in her hand. The chipmunks barely had enough time to wonder how that was possible, when Simon jumped out of the water right in front of them.

"Simone!" said Jeanette, relieved.

"Sorry if I caused you any worry, mademoiselle," said Simon with his usual extravagance. "Allow me to make it up to you." He held out a gold bracelet.

Jeanette couldn't believe it! "It's beautiful! Where did you find it?"

"Yeah, it is beautiful. Where *did* you find it?" Zoe's eyes narrowed. She was studying Simon suspiciously.

"In a cave behind the waterfall," answered Simon. But he wasn't really paying attention to Zoe. He only had eyes for Jeanette. "I thought it would look nice on you, but now I realize that even the most perfect gem cannot compare to your beauty." He placed the bracelet on Jeanette's wrist.

"Awww!" gushed Jeanette.

"Awww!" said Eleanor.

"Awww!" said Theodore.

Only Zoe wasn't affected by the romance. "So were there any other bracelets?" she questioned

Simon. "Or necklaces? Or gold coins?"

Simon shrugged. "I do not know. By the time I found the bracelet, I had already been gone from my Jeanette far too long."

"Awww!" giggled Theodore again.

The chipmunks crowded around Jeanette to look at the beautiful gift. They didn't notice Zoe hurrying away through the jungle back to her camp.

"Guys, guys!" Zoe whispered excitedly to her various tennis balls and footballs and basketballs. "They found it! They found it!"

Zoe knelt down in the sand and started digging frantically until she'd uncovered a shovel. "And the best thing is, they have no idea what they found. They think it's just one bracelet." In her eyes was a mad gleam. "The rest is mine, all mine!"

Zoe froze, embarrassed, as she looked at the faces of the different balls staring back at her. "I'm sorry, guys. Ours, all ours!"

She laughed crazily. She was out of her mind.

Chapter 23

By the end of the day, Alvin was putting the finishing touches on his driftwood hut. It looked pretty good, if he said so himself. Now it was time to help poor Brittany. "Okay, Brit," he announced. "I'm all done. If you want, I can help get you started."

But then he saw Brittany's shelter.

It wasn't a hut. It was a masterpiece. Somehow Brittany had created this amazing tree house with different levels and rooms and an extension that connected to her hot spring. She'd even made her own hot tub!

"Whoa," said Alvin, awed. "You know, maybe you are kind of the smart one. That tree house is awesome."

"Thank you, Alvin," said Brittany. She knew she?d won. "And yours . . . is . . . well, you did your best. Anyway, no reason we can't be comfortable and stylish while we wait for Dave to show up, right?"

Alvin suddenly felt uncomfortable. He'd been thinking a lot about Dave. What was worse, he'd been thinking about how he'd treated Dave when they were onboard the cruise ship.

"Um, Brittany, I think I know why Dave hasn't come," he admitted.

"You do?" said Brittany eagerly. "Why?"

Alvin took a deep breath. "Because he's not even looking," he said.

"Alvin, why wouldn't he be looking for us?"

"Because I drive him crazy. You know the way Simon's been driving me crazy? That's what I've been doing to Dave. For years. No wonder he hates me." He sat down in the sand, more depressed than he'd ever been.

But Brittany refused to accept this. "What do you mean? Dave's not coming for us? We're stuck here forever?"

Alvin put his head in his hands. He knew it was true. And it was his fault.

Brittany actually felt sorry for Alvin. "Don't worry, Alvin," she said, more sweetly than usual. "I'm sure Dave will come. I mean, he certainly loves Simon and Theodore."

Alvin sighed.

Neither Alvin nor Brittany realized that Theodore had been walking by at just that moment—and had heard everything. He scampered through the jungle looking for Simon and finally found him as night was falling.

The stars were coming out, and Simon was gazing up at them as Theodore, clearly upset, ran up to him.

He had tears in his eyes. "Simon? Is Dave ever going to find us?"

Simon didn't respond.

"Simon?"

Again there was no response.

And then Theodore figured out the problem. "Simone?" he said, trying to sound French.

"I'm sorry, were you speaking to me?" Simon said at once.

"Yes! About Dave! Where is he?"

"I see you are sad, *mon ami*, my friend," sympathized Simon. "And I hate to see you sad. I shall make it my business to find this Dave friend of yours."

"You really think you can find him?" asked Theodore.

"I know I can!"

Theodore looked so relieved. Everything was going to be okay.

"And then," said Simon, "I will find this Simon you keep speaking of!"

This was getting worse and worse! What were they going to do?

Chapter 24

Zoe kept glancing left and right to make sure no one was following her. In one hand she held a shovel, and in the other, a torch that gave off just enough light for her to make her way around the ledge by the pool to the waterfall. She slipped behind the wall of water and saw the entrance to the cave glowing green in the darkness. But the pile of rocks in front of the entrance blocked her way. She tried to pull out the boulders, but they were too big. She tried to use her shovel as a wedge, but she wasn't strong enough. She tried to squeeze herself between the cracks, but she was too big. There was no way into the cave where the treasure was hidden. Unless you were really, really small.

Only a chipmunk could reach the treasure.

Chapter 25

Another day dawned as Simon and Theodore searched the jungle.

"As Dave and I have never met, I will need you to describe him for me," Simon said.

Theodore thought hard. "He's very kind and a good storyteller." He paused and then scampered up a tree and held out his hand. "And he's about this tall."

"Mmm, very helpful," said Simon, peering at the jungle floor. "Is he by chance a large, flightless bird?"

"I don't think so," said Theodore. He was pretty sure Dave was just a guy.

Simon sighed and straightened up. "Then these

footprints are not his." He pointed at the large web-footed prints in the mud. They looked like they could have been made by a giant pelican.

"Jungle Monster!" screamed Theodore.

Not too far away, Dave and Ian were also slogging through the brush.

"Did you hear something?" asked Dave, listening.

"Yeah, my stomach grumbling," Ian answered.

"No," said Dave. "Maybe it was a helicopter. Listen!"

Ian's stomach grumbled.

"Face it, Dave: No one's coming for us. My stomach noises are going to get louder and louder and louder, until one day they finally stop. Because I will have eaten you."

"Maybe you're right," said Dave hopelessly. "Maybe no one's coming. Maybe the chipmunks aren't here at all. Maybe they're gone." He sighed. "I really messed up. You may as well eat me now."

"Hey, Dave," said Ian. "Okay, it kills me, kills me to say this, but you did nothing wrong. You're really good with those kids, and they really love you. And

I should know because I was really bad with them, and they really hated me. Whatever happens next, you should know you did nothing wrong."

It was the first nice thing Ian had ever said to Dave. He was touched. "Thanks." Dave smiled.

"Now come here," said Ian, holding out his arms for a hug.

Dave leaned in. He and Ian were becoming friends at long last. And then Ian lunged for his necklace. The string tightened around Dave's neck, choking him. Ian gnawed on the raw macaroni like a wild animal. Dave struggled to get loose, making the trees and shrubs around them shake.

On the other side, Theodore noticed the commotion. "The jungle monster! It's real! And it's angry!" He was scared.

"Or hungry!" said Simon. Which was even scarier.

Chapter 26

After all her work on the tree house, Brittany was ready for a nice steamy bath in her hot tub. She was going to wash her fur and get all clean and relaxed. She stepped into the water and immediately jumped out, screaming. It was boiling hot. Actually boiling. Scalding. What was going on?

And then she got it.

She looked up at the mountain looming over the island.

It was a volcano. And it was about to blow!

She called out to Alvin, Jeanette, and Eleanor to tell them what was happening. Simon and

Theodore were still somewhere in the jungle on the hunt for Dave.

"A volcano?" said Jeanette.

"Are you sure?" asked Alvin.

"That's why the water was so hot!" exclaimed Brittany. "It's being heated by the underground magma chamber!"

Jeanette was surprised. She didn't think Brittany would know something so scientific. "How do you know that?"

Brittany shrugged. "I have no idea! The place where I get my nails done always has the Science Channel on. Maybe I accidentally paid attention."

Zoe ambled over to where all the chipmunks were chattering. "Hey, anyone small up for a little hike? Maybe to the waterfall?" She was making an effort to be casual.

"Not now, Zoe!" said Alvin. The whole island's going to explode!"

Zoe looked horrified. "*What?* No, it can't. Not now. Not after all this time. . . ."

Zoe realized that she'd nearly spilled her secret. She recovered as quickly as she could. "Not after all this time that I've enjoyed living here."

"Guys," said Alvin, taking charge. "We need to get off this island. Fast. We have to build a raft—now."

Zoe was frustrated. "Like, right now? Or like, right after a quick hike to the waterfall now?"

The island began to tremble. More smoke billowed out of the volcano. There was no time to lose!

Chapter 27

Ian and Dave were still struggling over the macaroni necklace, when it finally snapped and went flying. Dave fell to the ground, Ian went scrambling into the bushes, and the necklace wrapped around Simon, taking him down.

"I've been hit!" he shouted.

Theodore rushed to his side and saw the necklace. "How did the monster get the necklace I made for Dave?" he wondered out loud.

A moment later he saw Dave still sprawled on the ground where he'd fallen during his fight with Ian.

"Dave?" asked Theodore. He couldn't believe it.

"Theodore!" exclaimed Dave, stunned. He

scooped the chipmunk up into a big hug, and Theodore reattached the necklace around Dave's neck.

Simon rushed over to them. "Dave? Ha-ha! I told you we'd find him!"

"Simon!" exclaimed Dave, wrapping him in a hug as well.

"It is Simone," said Simon stiffly. "But I am often confused for this Simon fellow. Perhaps we look alike?"

Puzzled, Dave turned to Theodore. But Theodore had just seen Ian. He looked as frightened as when he'd thought a jungle monster was after them.

"Don't worry, Theodore," said Dave reassuringly. "Nothing's going to happen to you. Is it, Ian?"

But at that exact moment the whole island began to tremble.

"What was that?" squeaked Theodore.

Smoke was billowing out of the mountain looming over the island. The rotten-egg smell of sulfur was in the air. "Oh, just an active volcano," said Ian.

Dave and the chipmunks exchanged terrified glances. They had to get off the island—fast!

Chapter 28

Alvin, Brittany, Jeanette, and Eleanor were gathering up bamboo as fast as they could to make a raft. Zoe watched from a distance, plotting something.

Alvin was directing the whole operation. "Okay, Brittany and I will build the deck. Eleanor, you need to start braiding ropes. Jeanette? Who knows how long we'll be out there, so find as many coconuts and mangoes as you can."

Dave, who had just been led into the clearing by Simon and Theodore, looked on proudly. He waited a moment, pleased with how responsible Alvin was being, and then spoke. "What can I do to help?"

The girls whirled around, and Jeanette and Brittany rushed into Dave's arms. Eleanor hobbled over on her crutches.

"Eleanor! What happened?" asked Dave, concerned, as he held Jeanette and Brittany close in a hug.

"I'm okay, Dave," she chirped. "It was just a zipline accident."

"A what?" exclaimed Dave, horrified. But then he caught himself. After all, maybe he needed to be a little less uptight. "Doesn't matter. The important thing is that you guys are safe."

Dave noticed Alvin was hanging back, staring at him.

"Alvin?" questioned Dave.

Alvin nodded.

"Everything's gonna be okay," said Dave reassuringly.

Alvin nodded again, his lower lip quivering. Dave knelt down next to him. "Hey, what is it?"

And that was all it took. Tears spilled out of Alvin's brown eyes. He'd been trying so hard to keep it together, to take care of everyone, to be a grown-up, but now that Dave was here he could be a little chipmunk again. He couldn't stop crying. "I thought you'd never find us! That you weren't even looking!"

Dave scooped him up into his arms. "What? Why wouldn't I look for you?"

"Because I'm such a pain in the—"

Dave stopped him with a look before he could say a bad word.

Alvin began again. "I know, you don't think I'm a pain in the—"

"Oh no," interrupted Dave, laughing. "You are. But I'd come no matter what." He hugged Alvin close.

Ian had been keeping an eye on the volcano. "Hey, what do you say we save the 'everything's okay' hugs for when everything's actually okay?"

Alvin couldn't believe it. It was Ian. What was he doing here? "Dave?"

"Kind of a long story," said Dave. There clearly wasn't time for it right now.

"So, how do we get out of here, Dave?" asked Alvin, wiping his eyes and getting serious again.

"I think you've got this under control," said Dave, pointing at the raft, which was almost finished.

Alvin smiled proudly. He jumped out of Dave's arms and began giving orders again.

"Theodore, you and Eleanor are on rope duty. Dave and Ian, we need oars. Simone, you and Jeanette are in charge of food. Zoe . . ."

"I know, go pack up my balls!" said Zoe, and she disappeared into the jungle.

Dave scratched his head, puzzled. "Who is that?"

"Another long story," chirped Theodore.

Chapter 29

Jeanette and Simon were gathering mangoes and coconuts to take with them on the raft when they heard heavy breathing from behind a bush.

"Did you hear something?" whispered Jeanette.

"When I am with you, all I can hear is the beating of my own heart," gushed Simon.

"Oh, Simone." As Jeanette swatted him playfully, a golf ball flew through the air and smashed into Simon's face, knocking him out.

Jeanette spun around and saw the basketball rolling toward her. She started to run, but it kept gaining on her, and as she looked over her shoulder to see how close it was, she tripped and fell into a hole.

The basketball rolled over the hole and stopped, trapping Jeanette beneath it.

Back on the beach, the others were admiring the raft they'd built. It was floating in the shallow water with oars made out of bamboo and the feet from Ian's pelican costume.

"It's incredible," said Dave enthusiastically. "And watching everyone work together to build it. I just want to say—"

But the rumbling volcano interrupted him. The whole island was starting to shake.

"It can wait," said Dave hastily.

They were about to climb onto the raft when Eleanor realized that Jeanette and Simon were missing. Everyone began frantically searching for them.

It was Alvin who discovered Simon knocked out in the jungle a few feet from the beach. "Guys! Guys! Over here!" he shouted.

"Simone, are you okay? Simone!" said Theodore, shaking him.

Simon blinked open his eyes. "Why are you calling me *Simone*?"

"Simon?" asked Alvin carefully.

"Uh, yeah."

"You're back!" cheered Alvin. "It finally wore off!"

"What wore off?" Simon adjusted his glasses and sat up.

Alvin explained. "You were bitten by a spider. It, like, messed up your brain."

Simon nodded, looking around. "Is that why I think I see Dave and a half Ian, half bird?"

Dave tenderly picked up Simon. "No, it's really me. And really Ian."

"'Sup," said Ian, trying to act cool. He held out his hand, but Simon just stared at him, still bewildered.

"Simon, where's Jeanette?" asked Alvin, who was keeping an eye on the volcano. "She was out here with you."

Simon looked more confused than ever. "I don't know."

"I do," said Brittany. She'd spotted the basket-ball lying on the ground. "It's Zoe. She took her.

Simon, I need to know where you found that gold bracelet."

This was all too much for Simon. He didn't have any idea what was going on. It was like waking up from a dream. "What gold bracelet?"

"The one you gave to Jeanette," said Brittany, exasperated.

"When did I give Jeanette a bracelet?"

Brittany was getting mad. "On your date!"

"Jeanette and I are dating?" Simon looked dazed.

"Okay, he's useless," sighed Brittany. "Theodore, Eleanor? You're going to have to lead the way."

"I don't remember exactly how to get there," said Theodore.

"I do!" piped up Eleanor. She was thrilled to finally be of use.

Eleanor and Theodore clambered up onto Dave's shoulder and directed him through the jungle along the path to the waterfall. Everyone else followed behind.

When they came to the deep gorge with the rotted log for a bridge, Theodore hesitated. "Okay, we just have to cross here," said Eleanor.

Simon looked down into the gorge with the rapids hundreds of feet below. Then he looked at the old, rotted piece of wood. "Are you kidding? I can't do that."

"But Simon, you already did," said Theodore. He didn't tell him that he'd done it backward.

"No, I didn't. That was Simone, not me."

"But Simone is you," said Brittany. "He's in there somewhere. You just have to find him, and soon. Jeanette needs you."

That's what did it for Simon. Because no matter who he was or how he was behaving or what accent he was using, he had a pretty big crush on Jeanette. And he wasn't going to let anything bad happen to her. But then he looked over the edge of the precipice again. "No, I'm sorry, I can't do it."

Dave was thinking fast. They didn't have any time to lose. "Ian, take everyone else back to the raft. If the volcano blows before we make it back, you have to promise me you'll—"

"Leave without you?" interrupted Ian. "Got it." He picked up Eleanor and Theodore and began to run, with Brittany and Simon following behind him.

Alvin stayed put.

"Alvin?" questioned Dave.

"I'm coming with you, Dave."

"Absolutely not; it's too dangerous," said Dave, putting his foot down.

It was a standoff. "Remember I said someday I might need to disobey you? That someday is now."

Dave could see the determination in Alvin's eyes. He couldn't say no to that. "Let's go."

Alvin scampered across the log.

Dave took a deep breath, resolved not to look down, and slowly and carefully crossed over to the other side. They just had to hope the log would still be there when they came back.

Chapter 30

At the entrance to the cave behind the waterfall, Zoe was tying a rope to Jeanette. "You're not coming up until I have every last piece of that treasure."

The volcano was rumbling even louder now. The smell of burning filled the air as Zoe lowered Jeanette through a chipmunk-sized hole.

"But . . . but . . . the volcano's about to explode!" cried Jeanette desperately.

"Then you better hurry, hmm?"

After a few minutes, Jeanette called out from the cave. "Okay! Pull me up. I can't hold any more."

But Zoe didn't believe her. "If you can still talk, it means you haven't stuffed your cheeks yet!"

There was a rustling noise from within the cave, and Jeanette mumbled something.

"That's better," said Zoe. As she started pulling on the rope to bring her out, the island began shaking harder than ever. Finally, she managed to lift Jeanette out. The chipmunk's arms were filled with jewels—emeralds and diamonds and rubies and gold.

Zoe couldn't believe it. She'd been looking for this treasure for years and she'd found it at last!

"Zoe!" chirped a high-pitched voice.

She swung around and saw Alvin and Dave.

"Not another step," warned Zoe. She grabbed Jeanette and held her tightly in her hands.

Dave took a step forward and spoke softly. He could see at once how crazy Zoe was. "Easy, easy. Jeanette, are you okay?"

Jeanette spat out a few jewels. "I'm a little scared, and those earrings tasted awful."

"Zoe, you don't have to do this," said Alvin.

"I don't?" screamed Zoe. "I spent ten years

looking for this treasure. It's the whole reason I came to this stinking island!"

"So you didn't crash-land?" asked Alvin. "You made that whole thing up?"

"They said I was crazy," continued Zoe. "They said this map was a fake." She held up a worn and wrinkled piece of paper.

Alvin peered at it. "I think that's a place mat from a fish restaurant."

"That's right," exclaimed Zoe. "I was working at the Crusty Anchor as a waitress. One day, an old man came in, ordered the all-you-can-eat popcorn shrimp and an Arnold Palmer. He didn't have enough money to leave a tip. But he said he'd give me something far more valuable."

Zoe flipped the place mat over, and drawn in crayon on its back was a treasure map.

Zoe was ranting now. "I found it. And all those people who doubted me—my shift manager, Dave Henderson; my assistant shift manager, Dave Henderson Jr.—they were wrong!"

The island shook again, and Zoe lost her balance. The jewels flew everywhere. "No!" screamed Zoe.

Jeanette took advantage of the distraction to jump out of her arms.

"Run!" commanded Alvin.

And they ran. As fast as they could.

At the gorge, Jeanette suddenly froze in place. She couldn't move another step. She was still attached to the rope Zoe had put on her. Like a leash. Like a chain. She was trapped. Zoe was pulling on the rope, reeling her in.

"You're going back into that cave! You're gonna get more treasure. You hear me? *You hear me?*" Zoe was totally out of control at this point.

Jeanette was terrified. There was no escape. She was going to die in the cave when the volcano exploded.

But just at that moment a dashing chipmunk swung through the air on a vine, as if in slow motion.

"Simone!" said Jeanette.

"It's Simon!" yelled Simon, swooping Jeanette up into his arms.

But she was still attached to the rope, and now both of them were being dragged back toward Zoe. Simon tried desperately to untie Jeanette, but the knot was too tight. He tried to gnaw it, but it was too thick.

They were getting closer and closer to Zoe when a familiar voice rang out through the jungle. Al*vinnnn!* Dave was doing his familiar scream. Only for once he wasn't angry. He needed Alvin right now.

He reached into his pocket, grabbed the pocketknife he'd taken from Alvin on the cruise ship, and threw it to the chipmunk—who caught it effortlessly.

Alvin knew exactly what to do. He sliced through the rope, Zoe tumbled backward, and the chipmunks and Dave took off toward the beach.

"Go! Go!" shouted Dave as they ran. There was no time to lose!

There was a huge blast. The volcano spewed smoke and flames and ash into the sky.

Jeanette and Simon scurried across the log over the gorge. Alvin followed. And Dave brought up the rear. He'd just stepped onto the log when it crumbled and crashed to the rocks hundreds of feet below.

Dave's hands reached out and grabbed at the side of the cliff. He was hanging on for dear life over the gorge. The chipmunks on the other side looked back in horror. "Hold on, Dave! You can make it!"

And then a shadow loomed over him. It was Zoe. And her feet were inches away from Dave's fingers.

Chapter 31

Ian, Theodore, Brittany, and Eleanor were waiting on the raft in the shallow water. Pieces of ash and soot filled the air. Embers were landing on the deck and threatening to light it on fire. They kept splashing seawater on them and anxiously looking toward the jungle. Where were the others?

"Look!" shouted Eleanor. She pointed as Alvin, Simon, and Jeanette ran across the beach toward them. The chipmunks dived onto the raft.

"But where's Dave?" said Brittany, alarmed.

Dave was still hanging by his fingers over the gorge, and crazy Zoe was looming over him, her feet still just inches from his hands.

"Help me up!" begged Dave.

"What am I supposed to do now?" said Zoe, seemingly unaware of Dave's plight. "My treasure is gone."

"You can go back," said Dave.

"To the Crusty Anchor? Don't you think they've given my shifts away? All I had left were those jewels, and now they're gone forever. My life is ruined."

Zoe lifted up a foot and was about to step on Dave's fingers when she saw Ian coming toward her.

"I know it's tempting to blame Dave," Ian said to her. "I've been there. I wish I could get back all those years I spent plotting revenge. All that time wasted. All that energy wasted. All those pizzas I had delivered to his house wasted."

"That was you?" said Dave.

"Not now, Dave," said Ian, keeping his eyes on Zoe. "Yes, you could let him fall. And I could go back to the raft with the chipmunks and be their manager again, making tons of money. So really, I'm good either way. But let me tell you something. Hate, anger, regret—those weren't just the names of the members of a girl group I once signed. They were what consumed me. And at some point, you have to let go. . . ."

Zoe looked down at Dave's fingers.

"Not of Dave," Ian said quickly. "Of those emotions. Or not. I'm good either way."

What would Zoe do? Even she didn't know. But the volcano had begun to explode.

Large clumps of lava were crashing down on the beach when Ian, Zoe, and Dave finally appeared, running as fast as they could. They reached the beach! They were in the water. They hurled themselves onto the raft at the very last minute. Ian threw Dave an oar, and the two men began paddling as hard as they could.

Smoke was everywhere. The beach was now covered in hot lava. But they had made it.

When at last they were far enough away from the island to be safe, Zoe was the first to speak. She apologized at once to Jeanette. "I don't know what to say. I guess I was just so obsessed with the treasure, I kinda went a little crazy, huh? I'm really sorry. We all are." She had her precious balls in her hands, and she made them nod apologetically.

"Apology accepted," said Jeanette. She actually felt a little sorry for Zoe. She was just so nuts. After a moment, she pulled the bracelet off her wrist and offered it to her.

Zoe was unbelievably touched. "Really? Look, guys, it'll be a new beginning—for all of us."

Dunlop the tennis ball smiled. So did Jeanette. She turned to Simon. "I hope you don't mind. Simone gave it to me."

"It's okay," said Simon shyly, barely able to meet her eyes. "Even the most perfect gem cannot compare to your beauty."

Jeanette stared at Simon, amazed. Suddenly Simon realized what he'd just said. Maybe there was a little Simone in him after all! He smiled as Jeanette rested her head on his shoulder.

Alvin scampered over to Dave, who was rowing beside Ian. "Um, Dave?" he asked hesitantly.

"Yes, Alvin?"

"I just wanted to say, now that we're not all dead and all . . . sorry I was acting like a child on the ship and kinda ruined our family vacation."

Dave stopped paddling and looked at Alvin, impressed. "It's okay. Sometimes a racehorse just needs a little room to run." Simon had been right after all.

"That is very wise, Dave," said Alvin. "I like where your head's at." He held up a paw for a fist bump, and Dave tapped his fist to Alvin's and then pulled him in for a hug.

Ian's face fell. "What, no love for Uncle Ian?"

"You put us in cages!" squealed all the chipmunks together.

"Seriously? We're still talking about that? New topic. I just saved Dave's life."

Theodore's little face squished up as he thought. "Okay, but I'll be watching you, mister." He pointed to his eyes and then to Ian.

"Hey, Alvin, do you still have that pocketknife?" asked Dave.

"Sorry," said Alvin sheepishly. "I meant to give it back."

"No, I want you to keep it," said Dave, smiling.

Alvin couldn't believe it. "Really?"

"And maybe you can use it to signal that helicopter," said Dave, pointing to one he had just seen in the sky.

Everyone started cheering.

Alvin flipped open the blade of his knife and expertly began using the metal to reflect the sun. He flashed, "SOS."

Dave nodded to Alvin. He was really proud of him. He was some chipmunk.

Chapter 32

The spotlight hit the stage at the International Music Awards. The music began. Six high-pitched voices started singing. The crowd went wild! Simon harmonized with Jeanette. Theodore and Eleanor shared a microphone. And Alvin and Brittany, singing together at last, stole the show. The Chipmunks and The Chipettes were back—and they were better than ever!

Dave and Ian watched from the wings.

"It's good to be back, isn't it?" said Ian.

"It sure is," agreed Dave.

"And I don't just mean in a 'not stranded on

an island' kind of way. I mean, I'm back, Dave! Back in business! I just made a deal for Zoe to sell her story to Hollywood. Huge bidding war." He named the famous movie star who was going to play Zoe—and the rap artist he wanted to play himself.

"Actually, Mr. Hawke?" An almost unrecognizable woman interrupted him. It was Zoe. She was all cleaned up and wearing a trendy outfit. She looked great. She'd even washed her tennis ball, Dunlop. She was holding him—and a movie script. "I had a question about some of the dialogue. I really don't think Dunlop would say that."

In her hands Dunlop nodded in agreement. Ian smiled tightly.

Dave laughed out loud. "Welcome back, Ian!"

Onstage The Chipettes and The Chipmunks were rocking the house, but toward the end of a song, Alvin held up a hand to quiet the band. "I wanna send a shout-out to a very special person in my life. Without him, I wouldn't be here right now. I'm talking about my dad, Mr. Dave Seville!"

Dave waved from the wings, a little embarrassed.

"C'mon out, Dave!" urged Alvin.

Reluctantly, Dave stepped out onto the stage and into the spotlight. The crowd cheered. Dave waved shyly again.

"You and I, we've been through so much together, huh?" said Alvin. "You were there with me in the casino."

People in the audience were whispering to each other, surprised. What was a little chipmunk doing in a casino? Dave looked ashamed. "No, no, it's not what you think," he tried to explain.

But Alvin interrupted him. "You were there with me when I blew off the side of the ship on a kite."

There were more disapproving murmurs from the audience.

"That's really not how it was. I was asleep!" said Dave, trying to defend himself.

Someone in the audience gasped.

Alvin chuckled. "And who could forget when we almost fell off that rotten log bridge?"

Now Dave was mad. "Okay, that's enough, Alvin."

"But no words could ever express how it felt when you threw that knife at me!" Alvin squeaked.

The audience couldn't believe it.

And neither could Dave. Just when he thought things were going to be easy, Alvin was back, as mischievous as ever. Just like old times!

"Al*vinnnn*!" he shouted.